This book is a gift for you

_____

celebrating your birth on this day

WITHDRAWN

_____

in the year

_____

When You Were Born

Dianna Hutts Aston

illustrated by E. B. Lewis

CANDLEWICK PRESS
CAMBRIDGE, MASSACHUSETTS

Text copyright © 2004 by Dianna Hutts Aston
Illustrations copyright © 2004 by E. B. Lewis
Calligraphy by Judythe Sieck

First edition 2004

Library of Congress Cataloging-in-Publication Data

Aston, Dianna Hutts.
When you were born / Dianna Hutts Aston ; illustrated by E. B. Lewis. — 1st ed.
p.   cm.
Summary: A mother describes the joyful time of her baby's birth
and how it was celebrated by family and neighbors.
ISBN 0-7636-1438-6
[1. Babies—Fiction. 2. Mother and child—Fiction.]
I. Lewis, E. B., ill. II. Title.
PZ7.A8483 Wh 2004
[E]—dc21   2002073901

2 4 6 8 10 9 7 5 3 1

Printed in China

This book was typeset in Calligraphic 810.
The illustrations were done in watercolor and marker.

Candlewick Press
2067 Massachusetts Avenue
Cambridge, Massachusetts 02140

visit us at www.candlewick.com

To my husband, David,
and to my children, James and Elizabeth
D. H. A.

To the children, our future
E. B. L.

When you were born

you came quietly,

and with eyes deep as an ocean

you looked at me,

and I looked at you,

and I thought to myself,

I know you!

And my heart heard you say,

I know you!

In that moment

I knew

you were a gift

from God

and that I would love you

forever.

When you were born

your daddy

stroked your satin skin

and planted kisses

on your downy head,

your tiny nose,

your curled fist.

Your lips formed

an *oh* of wonder

as you watched his face

smiling at you,

and Daddy's heart

was filled with wonder too.

When you were born

 your grandmother

 sat among the pink snapdragons

 in the garden

 and held you in her arms.

 The light of morning

 shone gold and green

 through the leaves of the oaks

 as she sang to you

 the lullaby she had sung to me,

 so softly and sweetly

 even the birds listened.

When you were born

your grandfather

traced your face

with his fingertips and said,

This child is somebody important!

You squirmed

under his tickling fingertips,

and stretched and yawned,

then slept,

and all the while

your grandfather

cradled you in his arms

and rocked you gently,

while you dreamed

the secret dreams of babies.

When you were born

your uncle—

my baby brother all grown up—

took you in his hands,

hands that grasped footballs

and baseballs

with ease

but trembled

when they held you,

and his eyes

grew round

with amazement

and he whispered,

A baby is so small!

When you were born

    our dog, Bear,

    just a big puppy himself,

    wondered what you were,

    and he sniffed your cheeks,

    your fingers,

    your blankets.

    Then he found a spot nearby

    and sat there quietly,

    on guard.

When you were born

the neighborhood mothers

arrived at the front door,

bearing gifts

of chicken and dumplings

and fruit salad

and cherry cobbler.

The mothers

took turns cuddling you

as tenderly

as they would their own babies,

and then they gathered

in the kitchen

and remembered the time

their children were born.

When you were born

    the neighborhood children

    sat in a wiggling circle around you

    and whispered loudly,

    This is the cutest baby ever!

    They measured your feet

    with their hands

    and giggled

    at your itty-bitty toes

    and played

    This little piggy went to market . . .

    until a mother

    shooed them outside.

There,

    in the backyard,

    they helped your daddy

    plant a magnolia tree

    in your honor,

    and when its roots

    were covered with earth,

    they leaned on their shovels

    and imagined the tree

    growing tall

    and strong

    toward the sun.

When you were born

the world hummed

its everyday tune

of footsteps and voices,

engines and bells,

but here

in our home,

our souls

sang with joy.

Prayers of thanksgiving

for you,

our child,

flowed from deep inside us,

like water from a spring.

We asked the angels

to watch over you

all the days of your life,

and they listened,

as angels always do.

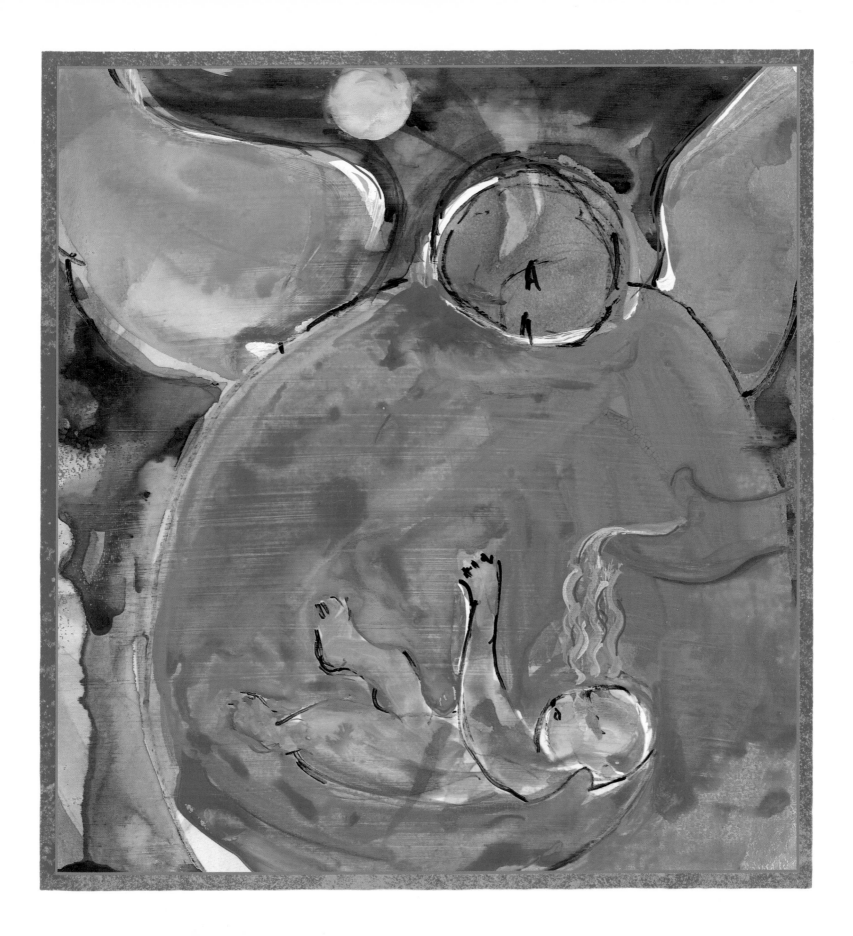